# TIN BOY

## STEVE COLE

WITH ILLUSTRATIONS BY
**ORIOL VIDAL**

*For Ailsa*

First published in 2019 in Great Britain by
Barrington Stoke Ltd
18 Walker Street, Edinburgh EH3 7LP

www.barringtonstoke.co.uk

Text © 2019 Steve Cole
Illustrations © 2019 Oriol Vidal

A CIP catalogue record for this book is available
from the British Library upon request

ISBN: 978-1-78112-872-5

Printed in China by Leo

# CONTENTS

# CHAPTER 1

# Deep Down

I don't want to go, but there isn't any choice.

At dawn we walk the worn path from our village to Rebo beach. The pontoons wait for us: rafts bound together with driftwood and reeds, plastic barrels, pipes and hoses, and hope. Soon we'll be out on the ocean, choking on the diesel smoke, the sound of the generator splitting our ears. We'll pitch from side to side as the sand is sucked from the seabed so it can be searched for fine black crystals.

This is what my family does, from youngest to eldest. We scavenge for tin. We dig into the land or the seabed, mining for tin ore. The world can't live without tin. Tin is used inside smartphones and laptops, cars and computers – things I'll never have. I wonder if anyone ever thinks where it comes from, this metal glue that makes their gadgets work ...

Or what we risk to get it.

I turn to Rustam, my uncle, who limps along beside me. "I don't want to go down into the water today," I say.

He grunts and tells me, "You must, Tono."

"But I'm only a kid – that's what you keep saying."

"You can work at your age," Rustam says, then adds, "And I can't go, can I? You want me dead like your old man? Who'll look after us all then?"

Rustam pushes me away, and I fall behind. I hate him. But I have to stay with Rustam, because Dad died and my mum left with my sister to find work. He doesn't really want me here, so I get the last of everything: food, clothes, kindness. Not that there's much to begin with.

Yan strides over the sand to join me. Yan is my cousin, and Rustam's son. He's almost a man now, and I share a room with him. He searches my face like he searches wet sand for tin. I know he's looking for tears. I won't show him any.

"Don't be scared, Tono," Yan says. He only has teeth on one side of his mouth, but he still smiles a lot. "No one's died in the mines for months. And I'll be near you."

"Can I have the wetsuit?" I ask him. "It's too small for you."

"And too big for you," Yan replies. "It'd flap about and slow you down." His tongue flicks over his broken teeth as always. "I know you wish you were some big deal in tights from those comics you read …"

"Superheroes," I say.

"Yeah, yeah. The titanic Tin Boy!" Yan laughs. "Just remember, the person's the hero, Tono. They change into the suit – the suit doesn't change them."

"Real deep, Yan."

He smiles again. "Not as deep down as we're going, Tin Boy."

I snort, trying to laugh it off.

Truth is, I do wish I could pretend to be somebody stronger. I look down at myself. No shirt. Scrawny stick legs. Pale cotton shorts held together by mud and stubbornness, like the rest of me.

The growl and sputter of the generators on the pontoons drowns out the sound of the ocean. Clouds of salt smoke and diesel blow across my face as I climb on board. Rustam and Yan push our raft out into the sea.

Yan puts on his wetsuit. It's grey where once it was black, and it's torn at the seams. He hands me my face mask as Rustam switches on the compressor, which blows dirty air down a plastic tube and into our lungs. A magic machine keeping us alive while we work. The whole pontoon trembles with the compressor's whine, and so do I.

The sea is busy with pontoons like ours. Then a deep sound blasts from the sky and we look past our rickety vessels to a giant ship – the dredger owned by a private mining company. The ship shakes as if it's laughing as it eats the world beneath the waves. Its bucketwheels bite deep down into the seabed, spitting out mud and swallowing the tin. What will be left for us?

I look in the water, but it's thick with sand. It shows no reflection, like I'm invisible.

Yan puts an arm around me and steps off the raft. I hardly have time to put the air tube to my lips as we trail down into the warm, silty water. In the scattered light I see dark and distant monsters – men or machines prodding at the seabed. My lungs ache as I suck on the tube and my breath leaves as bubbles.

My bare feet sink into the seabed. Yan crouches with the hose, which sucks at the thick sand. We have to make a ditch with our handmade tools, many metres deep. My job is to smooth the side of the ditch, trying to make it strong. As the minutes drift past, I imagine Rustam high above us, sorting through the debris as it sprays out through the hose. The

air up there is thick with fumes, but I still want it, so badly.

Sand swarms about my face like mosquitoes. The wall of the ditch towers over us now, maybe three metres high. It gets harder to see. My heart is thumping, and I'm chewing the end of the tube to breathe air that tastes of rubber. And still the ditch must go deeper. I search the mud wall for a trail of tin ore – there's a line of white rocks and soil you look for. If we're lucky, there'll be lots. We aren't lucky very often.

Suddenly I spot something in the sandy floor at my feet. Not tin. It's red and glints like there's light in it.

What the hell is that?

Yan grabs me by the arm as I stoop to scoop it up. My heart lurches, but it's OK – Yan's smiling and nodding. He's found a tin trail to follow, which means full bellies tonight!

He's still smiling as a crack opens in the ditch wall behind him.

I grab him and kick my feet to launch away, but the mud wall falls on me too fast. The tube jerks from my mouth, and I'm buried in an avalanche.

# CHAPTER 2

# Wake Up

I wake up slowly. There are flashes of light, like rays of sun in water. I am on a dirty mattress on the floor. My throat is raw and my chest's burning. My left hand is trapped in a fist; the fingers won't move. I can hardly breathe, and I think I'm going to be sick. The pain of it all makes me want to close my eyes and stay hiding in the dark. I don't know where I am or what's happened. I call out for my mum, then I remember Mum's far away in Belitung.

Someone in my head is screaming,
"*Longsor! Longsor!*" It means landslide. The
worst word you can hear.

I hear my dad's voice, but I only see a
crumbling, tumbling wall of mud. And suddenly
my feet are sinking into the seabed ... I'm
sinking all the way down as the mud and sand
fall and smother me—

"Hey."

It's a girl's voice, and I open my eyes to
crack the darkness, breathing fast. I'm in the
room I share with Yan in Rustam's crappy
house of clapboard and cinderblock. I stare
at the girl in front of me. Colours hit my eyes
first: plain blue T-shirt, yellow shorts. She's a
bit older than me, maybe fifteen. Spiky black
hair and brown frowning eyes. Have I seen her
before? The groove between her nose and her
lips looks like a perfect teardrop. I focus on
that, not sure if it's really there, or if she is, or
if I'm dreaming as I drown inside the seabed.

She shifts her feet. "You're staring."

"Sorry," I say.

"Normally people stare at *this*." The girl holds up her arm, and I see it ends just below the elbow. Two tiny finger-stubs push out from the stump, so I know she didn't lose her hand in a landslide. "I'm Kemala," the girl says. "I live in Sungai Liat."

That's the nearest town, ten kilometres away. I don't know why Kemala is here, but I don't care; I just want to sleep. My eyes flick to her other arm, which is all there, and I see what she's holding. Suddenly I'm cold.

Kemala has one of Dad's comics. *Amazing Spider-Man* issue 276.

I lick my dry, cracked lips. "Give that back," I say.

"It's good," Kemala says. "I haven't finished it yet—"

"Give." My voice is slurred, my tongue will hardly move, but she needs to know that Dad's superhero comics are just for me. He kept them his whole life – thirteen of them. They're falling apart, the covers are ragged and the staples have rusted away, but like the heroes inside, they won't quit.

I couldn't go to school cos Dad couldn't afford to send me. Dad wanted to invent things, but that cost money, and he thought illegal mining was the fastest way to get it. Turned out it was the fastest way to get him killed.

But I didn't need school anyway; I learned to read from the comics, the pictures helping me understand what the words must be saying. I used to "read" them out loud to Rinal, my little sister, when she was small. Rinal stared at me with such big eyes, full of wonder. The comics are special, and they made *me* feel special, and no one else can touch them.

So I bang my fist on the floor and say, "Give me it!"

"Calm down, Tono," Kemala replies. "I've been your nurse. Looking after you." She waves her stump with a shrug. "You'd be lying in your own mess if it wasn't for me."

I reach out to her with my left hand, but it's still a fist – it won't open. Then I see the tube in my arm. There's a bag lying on the table beside me. And there's another tube coming out from between my legs under what looks like ...

Oh my god, these shorts are padded. Like a nappy or something.

"There was an accident," Kemala says. "A big pit in the sea fell in on you."

I remember it now – the surge of sand in the water. The crushing weight of it. No breath. Darkness. "Yan," I say. "Yan, is he …?"

"You saved him." Kemala stares at me. I'm not sure if she's impressed or just confused. "You've been in a coma for five days."

I almost forget to breathe at all. "Five days …?"

"While you slept, the doctors pumped *tons* of mud from your lungs. You should be dead. People say it's a miracle you're not."

"My mum … did she come?"

"I don't think she even knows you were hurt."

Kemala's words stub out the tiny hope I had like a finished cigarette. It takes a while, but in the end I ask her, "Why would you look after me?"

"Your uncle asked around for someone to watch you," Kemala explains. "He said that if you died, that person could have all your things." She waves the comic at me and drops it by my mattress. "I really thought you were a goner. But I guess I'll stay on. I mean, you might get an infection. You could still die, right?" Kemala shudders and adds, "But you can wipe your own butt from now on, Tono. The doctor will be back tonight, and he'll take out that catheter ..."

Kemala goes on, prattling in a sing-song voice that fills my head in this hot, musty room. My left hand is edging open slowly. Something glints in my palm.

All this time, I was gripping hold of a stone. It's red and oval, a crystal or something, worn smooth. Lying in my twitching hand.

Kemala stares at the stone. "What is that ...? Glass or something?"

The stone seems to glow in the dim light through the shutters on the window.

"It's something," I say.

# CHAPTER 3

# Remember

"Alive, awake and unharmed," Yan says that evening with his gap-toothed grin. "Half the seabed falls on you, and not a scratch. You really *are* the titanic Tin Boy!"

"Fluke," Rustam snorts.

Kemala lingers by the door. "Miracle."

Yan winks at me. "Superhero."

I'm still holding the warm red stone in my hand. I say nothing.

"You saved me, Tin Boy," Yan goes on. "You grabbed me and gave me time to get clear."

Rustam shakes his head. "*You* dug Tono out from there, Yan," he says. "You're the hero."

"Well, you got him to shore, Father. You paid for the doctor."

"It nearly left me bankrupt," Rustam says with a sour face. "Still. Tono will pay me back, when he can work again."

I let out a long breath. It will be two weeks at least before I can go back to mining. The doctors said I should rest that long to be sure there are no complications from what happened. Rustam didn't argue, which surprised me. He even brought me some mango and a bottle of water.

"We need you back fast, Tono," Rustam goes on.

*Yeah*, I think, and I squeeze the stone in my fist. *You need your fool again to work the worst jobs.*

But that night, in our room, Yan tells me, "Father won't put you back on the seabed – not straight away at least."

My eyes widen in the dark. "Are you working down there alone?" I ask.

"For now, I have to. But I'll find someone who can help for a bit. Sure, we'll have to pay them. But I told Father expansion is a sign of success." Yan pauses, then adds, "Father's glad you're all right."

"He is?"

"Lying there with your eyes closed for so long, you reminded him of your dad after … you know. When your dad was lying in the house, waiting to be buried."

My throat feels as if I swallowed a baby's fist. It's three years since Dad died, and I was there when it happened, right there in the old pit in the forest, playing with Rinal. I know that the sides of the pit fell in, that the sand broke his bones and filled up his throat, but it's like the landslide buried my memories too. Next thing I remember is going back home and Mum holding me tight, but I could hardly feel her, not even when Rinal wormed into the hug too. We were all quiet for weeks or maybe months, and then Mum went to find work on our sister island, Belitung. Mum couldn't bear the mines any more. She took Rinal with her, cos Rinal was too young to leave alone, and I wound up here at Rustam's house.

"Does my mum know I've been sick?" I whisper to Yan in the dark. "Is she coming?"

"Father sent word," Yan says after a while. "If your mum could come back, I'm sure she would."

I think about this and slowly nod. "Mum must have a job. Her boss might not let her leave. And there's Rinal to think of."

"Yes. There is."

I think of Rinal too. She drove me crazy when we were together, but now she's gone …

I grip the stone tight, hard in my hand. I used to have a little blanket to hold at night, but Rinal has it now.

# CHAPTER 4

# A Glimpse of the Future

It feels so strange the next morning, when Yan gets up and dressed while I lie on my mattress. My chest is still tight and painful as I listen to Yan's and Rustam's steps and clatter. I'm sure that Rustam will burst in at any moment, his dark eyes glowering at me as he says, "Come on, you lazy halfwit. You've lain in bed long enough!" But they leave without saying a word, to join the others walking to the pontoons, thinking that I'm still asleep.

The house is so quiet. Have I ever been here alone? I hold my stone up to the light that creeps between the shutters. The crimson seems caught inside it like an ember.

Rustam looked at my stone yesterday, turned it over in his hands and declared it worthless. "Just glass," he said. "Bottom of an old beer bottle, worn smooth."

Yan didn't think so. He held it to the light and said, "Maybe it's like kryptonite. *Good* kryptonite."

I thought that kryptonite was a green rock that makes Superman weak, but Yan says there's red kryptonite too, which affects Superman in weird, unpredictable ways.

"Maybe this is Tin Boy's 'tinkanite'," Yan said, and laughed. "Whatever it is, this stone brought you luck. No wonder you didn't want to let go of it."

But Kemala didn't laugh. She just stood there by the door, her right hand cradling her stump of arm. The next time I looked, she'd slipped away.

Today, she arrives at our house at nine in the morning. "Can you walk, Tono?" Kemala asks.

"Of course I can walk." I get up slowly. "I feel fine. There's nothing wrong with me."

"You see? He survived unharmed," Kemala calls to someone in the yard. "He's coming out."

I'm frowning as I reach the door. Kemala has someone with her, hovering in our dusty yard. It's a woman with silver in her short black hair and lines baked hard into her face. She wears an old, faded dress and watches me.

"This is him," Kemala tells the woman. "The one they call Tin Boy."

"Tin Boy?" the woman says slowly.

I feel stupid and start to correct her. "My name is—"

"He's the boy who cheats death." Kemala cuts me off and smiles behind the woman's back. "I told you. See? He's real. The miracle boy."

The woman's eyes stay fixed on my face. "She says you found ... a stone."

It's true. I nod.

"It kept him safe," Kemala replies. She puts her fingers on my fist and opens my palm to show the woman my stone. "It's a magic charm. How else could he still live after the pit fell in on him?"

The woman reaches out for the stone. I snatch my hand away.

"Who are you?" I ask.

"I have three sons," the woman tells me. "One is dead now, from a fever. Aldan and Udi work a mine outside Sungai Liat." Water is rimming her eyes. "I had a dream. I saw them dead in a landslide."

"Just a dream," I say.

Kemala shakes her head gravely. "A peep at the future."

"The boys dig so deep," the woman adds. Her arms are folded tight, her nails plucking at her skin. "The sides of the pit are not terraced, it costs too much, takes too long. But if the sides fall in ..."

An image flashes into my head: my father in the pit, swinging a pickaxe, seven metres down in the ground. My mind is thrown from the image as words jump from my mouth: "Why are you telling me this?"

"Because she knows you can help her," Kemala says, "with your stone."

"What?"

"Look at him, just days after the sea pit fell in on him. Not a mark!" Kemala's words to the woman are slow but urgent. "Not a broken bone! The stone protected him; I'm telling you, it's magic. How else do you explain it?" Kemala sounds so sure. "This boy can stop your dream from coming true and keep Udi and Aldan from harm ... for just a small price."

A fragile smile grows on the woman's face like a flower rising from parched soil. "If my sons can truly be kept safe ..."

"The Tin Boy will come to you tomorrow," Kemala says.

"But they're digging now. In my dream I saw Aldan—"

"Tomorrow," Kemala insists. "I will walk back with you. We'll agree a price. Then tomorrow Tin Boy will come."

"Hold on," I say, taking Kemala by her good arm and leading her into the house. "What the hell?!" I hiss at her, once we're out of sight. "You think you're the boss of me? Why did you tell her all that stuff about—?"

"What I told her is true." Kemala grabs *me* by the arm now, and her deep brown eyes search mine. "You came back from the dead. Remember?"

"I was lucky."

"It was fate," Kemala says. "You found the stone." She nods. "You're not just Tono. You're Tin Boy now."

"And you're crazy. I'm ..." I pause and look at the dull red stone in my other hand. "I'm no superhero."

"You see how sad that woman is." Kemala lets go of my arm, suddenly angry with me. "Superheroes help people, don't they? Instead of sitting here, you could help her just by sitting on your butt out in Sungai Liat, watching her sons while they dig."

"And taking her money?"

"Expenses, that's all. You've got to pay back your uncle for the doctors, haven't you?"

I chew dead skin from my lip. Could Kemala be right?

It's incredible, impossible. But maybe the sea gave me back, and the stone saved my life, for a reason.

"What if the pit crashes in on her sons and I can't do anything?" I whisper.

"You *will*." Kemala speaks slowly and keeps eye contact, like I am a wild dog she's trying to tame. "I know you will."

It's scary but thrilling. I almost feel dizzy with it. The woman outside believes the dream that her sons will die, and she believes I am special. Kemala believes it too. If I get money, I can pay back Rustam quickly, so he will be happy with me for once ... and imagine what my mum will say! Won't she be amazed by her boy. By Tin Boy!

"You're going to do this," Kemala says, smiling. "Aren't you?"

# CHAPTER 5

# **The First Mission**

Every superhero has a story that explains how they became special. Superpowers can come from a spider bite, or some random accident, or scientific genius, or in a lightning bolt from the gods.

Whatever happens, it leaves them changed for ever.

I have a lot of time to think on these things as I sit on a dune, watching Aldan and Udi and their group. They're scavenging for tin in pits that have already been mined out by the private companies.  It's like a thousand other pits on this island.  It's like the pit where we lost Dad.

The miners break up the sand with water, then suck up this thick gritty soup using hoses. It sprays onto a sandbank, making a dirty

turquoise pool.  A pump pushes it into a special wooden trough where people wash and scrape the dirt to catch the tin ore that sinks to the bottom.

That was my life for so long, before Rustam switched us out to work the seabed.  And now …

I hold up the red stone to the sun and watch light and colour simmer there, like I've got a miniature sun in my hand.  My little sun shines across the dull, gritty sand dunes and the crater pools all around.  Its rays reach the tents and tarpaulins that shelter the scavengers, and the bits of forest still standing.  Dad said there used to be so much forest here, before the mines were dug.

There are other scavengers across the plain – I can hear their generator from here. Aldan and Udi must think I'm with that group. Their mother hasn't told them she is paying me to keep them safe from a bad dream.  They would think I was tricking her and be angry.

But I didn't ask her to hire me. I'm getting 25 cents today, just for sitting here. Better than lying on my mattress at home for nothing! I dream of what I could spend it on. Fruit or meat ... anything to eat that isn't soy beans and tofu. If I save for a long time, I could send money to my mother. Yan is learning to read and write, so I could ask him to tell her: *You don't have to slave in Belitung any more, Mum. Not any more.*

The hours pass as I sit on that dune, and sometimes my plans seem possible and sometimes they just seem stupid and crazy. How can I have any powers at all, really? Only a stupid little kid could think such a thing.

Then I remember something from before, from when Dad was alive: the day that a man came all the way from Belitung. He was from Walhi, the conservation group that helps the environment. He'd come to see illegal miners and had a special metal box that he waved around us.  The box crackled, and Walhi Man nodded.

"Do you know that the tin ore is radioactive?" he asked my parents.

I remember my heart sped up.  I knew about radiation from Dad's comics.  Spider-Man was bitten by a radioactive spider and it gave him powers.  Daredevil was blind but radiation made his other senses better.  And radiation made the Hulk strong and shiny green.

Could the radiation have done something to me too?  If Walhi Man waved his special box over my stone right now, would it buzz and shake with power and energy?

But Walhi Man talked about the radiation making people sick.  He said that by mining we were all risking our health.

"The biggest risk to our health is making no money," Dad said.  "If we don't get tin, we have nothing to sell.  If we have nothing to sell, we starve."

Today, with no tin, I am making 25 cents from sitting on this dune.  I could buy some sweets or a banana.  It's an amazing feeling.

I'm sitting in the shade and I'm tired, but I know I mustn't sleep.  I don't want anything bad to happen, and I don't really know how to stop it.  Will the stone help?  I could be sitting here for days.  What if the radiation wears off?  What if it's already gone – or was never even there?  Rustam will want me back working on the raft in two weeks, and what happens then?

It's like in the comics – there's always a "To Be Continued" box when the story runs out of space.  You had to wait just a month or so to find out what happened next.  But I've been waiting my whole life.

# CHAPTER 6

# The Titanic Tin Boy

In the afternoon Aldan and Udi's generator breaks down. It happened this morning, too, and took 30 minutes to fix. The same as on Rustam's raft, there's always something breaking down.

The men stand around the generator with tools, like surgeons fighting over who will operate on it. Then I hear the whine of a different engine. It sounds close by – the other miners must be moving closer. Maybe someone could ask them for help?

I close my eyes for a bit until I hear movement. It's only Kemala, picking her way across the mud from the pit towards me. Her clothes are muddy.

"Aldan and Udi still alive, huh?" she says, pointing to the huddle of men. "Good job."

"I've done nothing," I say, and nod to her filthy clothes. "What did you do?"

"Slipped into one of those crater pools this morning while I was checking out the place. I lose balance sometimes." Kemala holds up her arm stump, which is caked in dried mud, and goes on: "I heard Aldan talk to Udi at lunch-time. They thought they might make four dollars each today."

"Four!" I'm impressed; Rustam says it's a good day if he earns three, and that's still double what he used to make as a fisherman. "Do you think the woman will want me back here tomorrow?"

"Sure. Good sons give money to their mother. And a good mother will pass money on to you."

At the generator, Aldan straightens, and the machine splutters like a sick man coughing up his guts. The engine note holds, and there are cheers from Udi and the others. Aldan pretends to bow, then heads back to the pit.

That's when I see it, maybe eight metres above Aldan – a crack splitting open in the wet mud and sand.

Time slows. I picture my dad at the bottom of his pit, and I see the tide of sand and mud crash down and snuff him out. A single second and Dad's crushed. Then the flash of this vision is gone: my father's time has caught up to Aldan's.

Aldan hasn't seen the split in the sand like a widening smile. He's stepping into the pit.

"No!" The word screams from my lungs as I tilt forward and throw myself down the steep slope. "Landslide! Get out, *get out!*"

Aldan looks up and sees his death. I'm skidding and rolling down the slide.

A blare of shouting. The pit caves in.

I close my eyes.

When they open, I'm gripping on to Aldan's arm. The rest of him is buried in muck. His friends are shouting, digging with hands and pails. Frantic.

"He's squeezing my arm!" I say, pulling on his wrist. "He's still alive. Hurry!" Then the sand moves. I'm pulling him out. *I'm actually pulling him out.* Aldan's head emerges, muddy clods clinging to his hair and skin. Then I'm pushed aside, my hold broken as Udi and the others pile in. There's a rush and a push and Aldan is delivered fully from the pit, screaming.

His left leg is twisted badly. Purple-black
streaks ripen under the skin.

"That kid saved his life!" one of the men
says, pointing at me. I'm in such shock I don't
know what to do or say; I just sit there in the
mud panting for breath. Where's Kemala? I
can't see her at the top of the dune. Where did
she go?

The men lift Aldan onto a table. He's stopped screaming; he's just sobbing with the pain now. He'll be all right. Udi appears beside me and grips my hand. "Thank you," Udi says, over and over. He runs to join his friends who are already turning a tarpaulin and long branches from a lean-to into a stretcher.

Then I see Kemala is back and she's fetched the boys' mother. The woman slips and stumbles down the slope in her haste to reach Aldan. Once she sees he is all right she turns to me, tears on her face, and she holds me the way my mum used to, years back. "Thank you, Tin Boy," she murmurs. Too soon the holding is gone and the woman's pushing money into my hands. "Thank you."

Kemala takes over and leads me by the arm, away from the fuss and shouting. "Come on. It's over." Some coins spill from my palms as I go, and Kemala snatches them from the sand.

"Did you see? I saved him," I say. I'm still dazed, can't believe what has happened. "The woman saw the accident in her dream, and it nearly came true, but I stopped it."

"Fate. I knew you would do it," Kemala says. "Tin Boy is going to be famous."

"Famous?" I ask.

"The woman will tell anyone she meets." Kemala looks at the coins she's picked up. "You wait. Everyone's going to be talking about Tin Boy."

# CHAPTER 7

# **Word Spreads**

Kemala is right, and I have my proof the next night.

Rustam takes me with him to the collector, who buys tin from scavengers like us and sells it on to the private melters.  Yan would go normally, but his chest is bad today.  Breathing fumes from the compressor makes you sick, plus he swallowed a lot of seawater.

The collector weighs our tin ore on the scales, moving brass weights along a beam to balance it out.

"We gathered five kilos today," Rustam told me on the walk here. "The price last week was only three dollars per kilo. If it's any lower, I will not deal. By the time I've covered wages and expenses ..." He trails off, his face darkening. "The price must rise. It has to."

The price of tin would be higher if it was only the private companies who supplied the melters, but with all the extra tin from the illegal mines, the price stays low. The big companies that need all this tin to make phones and tablets and things don't want to pay any more, cos their customers want everything cheap. So the traders can't pay the melters much, and the melters can't pay the collectors much. At the bottom of the pile, there we are. We risk our lives for the tin they all depend on, and we get the least of all.

Still, today I am rich because the woman gave me a whole dollar, way more than she promised, because she was so happy. If not for me, her son would be dead. I gave a quarter of the dollar to Kemala because this was her idea and because she took care of me when I was in the coma. And because if she hadn't believed in me, I would never have believed in myself. I've hidden the 75 cents under my mattress with my red crystal. It's more riches than I've ever known.

I'm thinking of how I could spend it, or how I could save it. Or if maybe I should've asked for even more. And that's when I hear people in the street, drinking around a burning trash can:

"This kid, he's like a magic charm. He saved a ton of people when a pit fell in."

"I heard! That Tin Boy dude?"

"That's him! They say he was buried in mud and found a jewel that fell out of the sky. Wherever he goes, it keeps you safe."

"The hell it does.  Who is he?"

"There's a girl with one arm, she's the only one who knows how to find him.  I heard this woman talk – Tin Boy watches your pit, and no more accidents."

"Screw digging for tin, man, let's dig us up a sky jewel and get some of that action!"

And they laugh, and my cheeks burn, and I can't believe what I'm hearing, or how the story has spread and grown.  Meanwhile, Rustam and the collector are arguing beside me:

"The ore's not pure."

"If you don't take it, I'll sell it elsewhere."

"It's not fine enough.  I can only go to two dollars fifty a kilo."

"You can only go to hell …!"

And I wish I could shut out their argument –
the same one they had last week and the same
one they'll have next week. I want to just listen
to the men around the fire as they talk about
me. Me! This must be how Peter Parker feels
when he hears people in New York City talk
about Spider-Man.

Rustam turns his back on the collector,
swears and swings the bag of ore onto his back.
So we'll be walking across town to the next
collector. The men have stopped talking about
Tin Boy, but I'm replaying the conversation in
my head. I can't wait to find Kemala tomorrow
and tell her she was right about the way word
has got around.

Then I realise that I don't even know where
Kemala lives.

# CHAPTER 8

# A Ride to the Beach

Kemala calls for me the next morning after Rustam and Yan leave, Yan still coughing and feeling sick. I feel bad Yan has to go down beneath the waves again. I feel all right, better than him for sure.

I'm looking under the mattress at the money and the jewel when Kemala bounds up, banging on my open door with her arm stump. I jump away quickly. She looks out of breath. Her yellow skirt is caked in dirt and swings around her peg-doll legs; I guess she fell on the way over. But her eyes are shining.

I can't wait to tell her about last night. "Kemala, you won't believe what—"

"You've got to hurry," she breaks in, "I got you more work. Pontoon north of Rebo beach. It's some kid's first day mining the seabed, and his old grandfather wants him protected."

I can't believe what I'm hearing. "His granddad heard about Tin Boy ...?"

"He's *paying* for Tin Boy! So get your rock and your special powers and come on, Tono. No, wait." Kemala reaches behind her with her good arm and pulls something from the back of her waistband. It's a pair of blue shorts. They look almost new, not threadbare like mine. She throws them to me. "Put these on. You should look smarter."

I stare. The blue is a shade of the ocean. Wearing these shorts, it's as if I have a costume at last.

"Go on, then," Kemala says.

I frown, embarrassed. "Don't watch!"

"Who changed your coma pants and wiped your butt, superhero – you think I haven't seen all you've got?" Kemala laughs and turns her back. "Get on with it."

I kick off my old shorts. The new ones feel so soft as I slide them up. The lining of the pockets is strong; the stone slips in and stays there. "What about Rustam though? If he sees me …"

Kemala doesn't turn back round. "Don't worry, this pontoon works the coast a mile north of your uncle's patch. I found a bike so we can get there faster." I notice the scratches on her arms, and now I get why she's muddy:

riding the tracks one-handed can't be easy. "You'll be better at riding the stupid thing," Kemala adds as if reading my thoughts. "I'll sit behind you and tell you the way."

"Deal," I say.

I follow Kemala out to the bike – not much more than a rusting squeak. She got it here, all this way? I realise how determined she is. How much she believes in me.

I pedal fast, following the highway, the tarmac winding past mosques and mangroves and cinderblock houses in busy clusters. Beyond them, sand stretches out, and the buses and trucks thundering past whip sand into our faces. But Kemala's good arm is around me, and she laughs as we fly over the bumps on our wonky wheels. And I feel full of strength, as if something inside me has woken now, just like I did after the five days of dark.

*

I have to wheel the bike over the last stretch
of sand. Kemala has pointed out an old man
sitting cross-legged on the beach. He's scooping
up sand with a plastic plate and searching it
for precious grains of tin. He's too old to work
on the raft – that must be why his grandson's
started – but he's still trying to contribute.

The old man stands slowly as we approach.
He looks me up and down and asks to see
the stone. I hold it up to the sun. The light
reflects on his face and he turns away, nodding,
pointing out to sea. The raft is only a few
hundred metres from the shore.

"You can swim it," Kemala says.

I know I can. Easy. But I feel sick, smelling
the diesel wafting over the waves, hearing that
rumble of motors. In my mind I am back in the
water with Yan as the mud mountain collapses

over me. I try to take a deep breath and put my foot in the water, but I snatch it back out like I've touched acid.

"What's wrong with you?" Kemala's voice is low. "You must go. You are strong. You're Tin Boy, and someone needs your help."

I look down at my new shorts, the same colour as the sea. This ocean could've broken me, but it gave me the stone. It gave me strength.

"You're not going to sink beneath the waves and the mud," Kemala says with her hand on my arm, speaking softly. "All you have to do is sit on the raft and watch the old man's grandson."

"Watch *over* him," I say.

"Yes." Kemala's little arm presses against my chest, nudging me backwards. "Go watch over his grandson, Tin Boy."

And the old man is looking over, and I don't want to seem weak in front of Kemala. I turn and close my eyes and wade into the water, and when it's up to my neck I swim for the raft. I keep the stone tight in one fist. I keep swimming.

# CHAPTER 9

# Someone in Trouble

I pull myself out of the water and onto the rickety pontoon. There are four men on the raft, all dark and lean. No one smiles or welcomes me. They look across to the old man on the shore and mutter about how he's lost his mind.

The raft is in worse shape than Rustam's. It tilts to one side. Gaps in the branches are stuffed with rope and cloth, and the generator is old – it whines like an old man on his deathbed. I sit near the side of the raft. I see

the compressor and air tubes snaking into the water.  Three people are working down there – I see them as they bob to the surface, gulping down air.  Two men of Yan's age and a boy closer to mine.  The boy, Dulak, is breathing faster and deeper than the others.  I see the fear behind his eyes, the fear I felt myself.  I try to smile at him the way Yan smiled at me – *I'm here, you're all right now* – but this boy won't look at me.  I guess he's embarrassed; he doesn't want me here.  Only the old man back on the beach wants me here.

I begin to feel stupid.  My new shorts itch.  At lunch-time the others share food around but leave me out.  They tease Dulak and flash me glances.  And as the day drags on they get bolder:

"Not sharing with your guardian angel, Dulak?  Well, how can a Tin Boy be hungry, huh?"

"If he's thirsty, he can drink seawater. That's why he's here – he drowns so you don't have to."

They laugh, and I want to tell them all to go to hell, but I know that's not what heroes do. Everyone believes Spider-Man is a menace, but he doesn't get mad at them. He goes on protecting them just the same.

The men start laughing about a girl with one arm and her bad dancing. Across the rippling waters I see Kemala jumping up and down, waving her arm, maybe ten metres from where the old man sits by his puddle of seawater.

Fear bites in my belly. Something's wrong. Something's happened.

I squint from the side of the battered old raft. Kemala's beckoning me, her movements urgent. I turn to the kid I'm meant to be watching over. "I'm sorry, I think I'm needed."

Dulak looks away. "Not here."

I hesitate, feeling foolish. Then I dive into the water. For a moment I fear the grit, sand and salt will hold me under the waves, stop me from rising for air. But I break the surface of the filthy water, and I keep swimming. Kemala is watching. I want to show her how fast I can get to her. I will find out whatever is wrong and then go back to the raft, even if they don't want me there. The old man has asked me; I'm doing it for him.

Kemala splashes up to me as I crawl out from the water, the oil over my limbs shining rainbows.

"The old man lied to me," Kemala says. She seems furious, almost snarling. "He can't pay! He has maybe ten cents when he promised a dollar a day. We're not staying."

"What?" I look back to the raft. "But if we agreed to do it ..."

"If it gets around that Tin Boy shows up for ten cents, we – *you* – will be a joke. You want people laughing at you?"

The men on the raft already had laughed at me. I look at the old man. He holds his plastic plate and stares back at me, sadly. He looks so defeated. "Kemala," I say, "if ten cents is all he can afford, maybe I could …?"

"We're going," Kemala insists.

The old man starts to beg, holding out the filthy coins in his filthy hands, but Kemala tells him no. She tries to pick up the bike with her one good hand. I have to help her, and she stalks away, leaving me to it. I wheel it over the sand after her, and the old man's cries are soon too hoarse to rise over the roar of the generators. I look back and Dulak's pontoon is just one of a hundred turning on the water.

# CHAPTER 10

# Tin Dents

"There are other people who need Tin Boy," Kemala tells me as we reach Sungai Liat. "I will see who deserves you the most and come tomorrow if they check out."

By "check out" she means check if they can afford it. I look at this girl who guides me and realise I know next to nothing about her. "Shall I drop you to your house?" I ask.

"No," Kemala says, and then kicks the bike. "I'm not getting back on this heap of rust."

"You were the one who found it!"

"Yeah, and you're welcome to it."

"Who do you live with?" I ask her. "I don't even know."

"It's just me. I'll see you tomorrow."

She sets off, walking past the clapboard shacks, a crowd of skinny hens parting as she passes. *There's a girl with one arm, she's the only one who knows how to find him*, the man in town had said last night. It's a nice touch – like, only Rick Jones could get hold of the Hulk or Captain Marvel, I think. Rick even became a kind of honorary Avenger.

Yeah, Kemala knows how to find me. But I feel as if she doesn't want me to find her.

I cycle home, the bike whooping and squealing with each turn of the pedals. I hide it in a vacant yard a little way from Rustam's house, under some dusty brown palm leaves.  I don't think anyone will steal it, but I don't want Rustam to know I've got a bike.

I get back and it's mid-afternoon.  I go to change out of my shorts and put on my old ones.

I start when I see that Yan is here in our room, lying down on his mattress.

"Hey, Tono."  Yan props himself up on one elbow.  "You've been gone a long time."

"I went for a walk," I lie.  "Why are you here?  Are you OK?"

"Just an infection, I think.  That stinking air we have to breathe.  I'll be fine tomorrow."  Yan coughs, and his whole body shakes, as if set for mutiny.  "Nice shorts, by the way.  New?"

"I ... found them," I say.

"On your long walk.  Right."  Yan lies back on the bed, not so much because he's tired, more like he doesn't want to look at me any more.  "I heard talk in town, Tono.  About a living miracle called Tin Boy, available for hire to keep miners safe – if you can afford him."

I feel a jolt of dread inside.

"What do you think you're doing, Tono? Tricking people into giving you money ..."

Anger burns my throat.  "I'm not tricking anyone!"

"So it *is* you," Yan says.

I turn my back on him, swallowing hard. "Have you told your dad anything?" I ask.

"Don't be stupid.  But I called you Tin Boy for a joke.  *This* ... this is wrong."

"I'm not hurting anyone. I saved someone's life. This guy called Aldan, he would've died if not for me. *You'd* have died."

"I've thanked you, haven't I? D'you want me to pay you as well?"

"Now who's stupid?"

"Tono, listen," Yan says. "You only survived that landslide by a fluke. It's dumb luck the doctors could save you, that's all."

"You sound like your dad now. But maybe it wasn't luck. Maybe it was something else."

"Fate, you mean? Destiny? A lump of old glass turning you into a superhero?"

"Tin ore is radioactive," I tell him. "Maybe it affected me—"

"Radiation only kills you," Yan snaps. "Slower than a landslide but just as sure." He coughs again, shakes his head. "We dig away at our home, and our home digs away at us. Each hurting the other a little more every day."

I look at Yan and pull out the red stone. "Our home should've killed us. But I woke up without a scratch, with this in my hand."

"And now you're indestructible?"

"Maybe I've been made better."

"You've been made the same as the rest of us here," Yan says, "to risk your life each day mining cheap tin so that someone far away can afford the latest smartphone."

I shake my head. "So that we can eat."

"I guess you can eat what you want now, huh? If you're buying new clothes …"

"I didn't even buy the shorts," I say. But I think of the food I wanted to buy myself yesterday and feel a flash of guilt and anger. "You – you're jealous! That's what you are."

"Is that right." Yan's words aren't a question, and his eyes are dark as he stares me out across the stuffy room. "Well, just remember, Boy of Tin. Tin isn't so strong. It's a soft metal."

I've had enough. I turn and stomp out of the house.

"Tin dents easy!" Yan shouts after me.

# CHAPTER 11

# **Missing Person**

It's a sour atmosphere that night in the house. Rustam's been drinking, and he snaps and spits every time he opens his mouth. He's been let down by me and Yan, he says. Both of us are no good to him. He's trying to keep us all afloat on his own.

"I asked all over for anyone who'd take your places for a few days," Rustam goes on as he sits on his seat – a crate laid with carpet – and swigs from a dirty glass bottle. "One of them refused unless I paid another boy too, to watch over them! Can you believe that? Apparently there's some crazy kid saying he can protect people."

Yan looks over at me. I bury my face in my father's tattered old *Tales of Suspense*, thinking of when the Red Skull gets hold of the Cosmic Cube, a jewel that gives him the power to do anything.

"The world's going mad," Rustam says, and stomps on a cockroach running across the floor. "It's all going to hell. And you, Tono? You do nothing all day but look at stupid kids' drawings. Men in tights." He spits on the crushed cockroach. "Superheroes!"

Saying nothing, I turn the page, even though I already know every detail of every panel I'll see. Captain America can't run from the Red Skull. The Skull's every wish can be granted by the Cosmic Cube. But Captain America gets lucky and knocks the glowing jewel from Red Skull's hand, and it sinks to the bottom of the sea where it's lost.

I wish it were morning.

*

When the sun rises, Yan does too, despite the fact he's still coughing. I'm glad. For most of the night I was thinking about how things might have gone if Rustam had asked more about this crazy miracle boy and found out it was me.

It's weird how life feels more dangerous now than it did when I risked my life in the water each day.

Perhaps because it feels like I have something to lose again.

Rustam says nothing, but thumps about the house. I guess his head must ache from all the drinking last night. Or maybe he just has nothing to say. I don't care, anyway.

Once they've gone I put on the blue shorts and wait for Kemala to arrive and tell me where I'm going next. I hope the old man on the beach isn't too sad about it.

But Kemala doesn't come.

I wait for her all morning; I look at my stone for the millionth time. Have I really come back from the dead with the power to save people, or is it all just dumb luck? What about Aldan, though? I saved him, I did.

It's almost twelve o'clock when I venture out. I check on the bike and it's just where I hid it. Besides the shorts I wear and the money under my mattress, it's the only solid thing to prove the last couple of days have been real. I pick the bike up and ride it as best I can, past the palms, churches and mangroves on the road to Sungai Liat. It's a lot easier with no Kemala holding on.

Screeching all the way, the bike takes me to where I left her yesterday. The scrawny chickens are still pecking the ground. I find a man sitting cross-legged on a mat outside his shack. I ask after Kemala and the man waves me west. I follow his wave and reach the outskirts of the town, where mosques with blue china roofs look down on assorted shacks of clapboard and cinderblock, and I don't know where to start. I feel stupid. What if Kemala has walked over to my place, and I missed her on the way?

Then I decide: I can wait for her at her place the way she waited for me. I just need to find out where she lives.

So I start asking around. I ask a young woman with two children clinging to her, sandy from the beach. I bother a builder laying tiles on a path. I quiz an old woman who's wearing a shawl despite the dripping heat. None of them are sure, but each has a different lead on where I could find this scowling girl with one arm they've seen about.

Finally, pushing the bike now, I come to a backstreet where the paving gives way to scrub, and stumps of palm trees die in the dust. Hovels of crumbling concrete are barely standing and covered in graffiti. Bad air blows across from a rubbish tip on the other side of the road, and a dog's high-pitched bark interrupts the growl of traffic. Two guys, older and bigger than me, are standing beside a battered skateboard. One is tall, with a skinny beard and a gold chain round his neck. His friend is stockier and wears a white bandana. They're taking it in turns to try to flip the skateboard into their hands by hitting one end with their heels. They can't do it.

I call to them, "You know if a girl with one arm lives here?"

Bandana Man stamps harder on the skateboard, which twitches and clatters. "Who's asking?" he says.

Warning bells sound off in my head. *You can't say what you're doing here.* "Uh ... my name's Rustam." It's the first name I think of, not my dad's, and that annoys me. "This girl, she nursed someone at my house. Now someone else wants to hire her."

Gold Chain just looks at me. "Good money in nursing, huh?"

I shrug and say, "Not really." I don't like the look of these guys. I don't want them to think Kemala's got anything worth stealing. "They just feed you while you're there."

"Same as in prison." Bandana Man smirks at his friend, then points to a house towards the end of the street. "You'll find her at the end, there."

I want to cheer, but I stay cool, nod thanks to the men and move on. I prop the bike against a crumbling wall. I can feel the guys' eyes on me as I peer into different dusty windows. I wish they'd get lost.

Finally, with a thump of triumph in my chest, I find Kemala sitting on the floor inside, her back to the window. The peeling wooden door to the side of the small house had a lock on it once, but it's been smashed off. I smile anyway, because this is perfect – it means I can do now what she normally does to me.

So I burst in through the door and say, "Look out!  It's your friendly neighbourhood Tin Boy ...!"

Kemala swears, throws the stub of her arm across her chest and with her right hand snatches up a rusty knife.  Little piles of money are placed around her on the matted floor.  I take in the clean yellow top and the neat black skirt she's wearing, and the look flashing over her fierce face that says "busted".

## CHAPTER 12

# Fight and Flight

"Whoa!" I say, and put my hands up to calm Kemala. "I didn't mean to scare you—"

"What are you doing here?" she demands. "How did you find me?"

"It wasn't easy."

"You shouldn't have come." Kemala puts down the knife at last. "This was my aunt's friend's place before the cops took her. No one's meant to know I'm here."

I'm just staring at the money. "Where did this come from?" I ask.

She shrugs. "Bookings."

"Bookings? For Tin Boy?"

"S'right. After that stupid old man tried to rip me off, I'm taking the money in advance." Kemala's shoulders relax as she scoops up the money in her palm. "I was coming to see you later today."

"I didn't know."

"Next job's not till tomorrow," Kemala says. "Old pit's opened up again, near a beach east of here."

I wish I hadn't come to her. I feel awkward, angry. "How much money have you been charging people?"

"What I can." Kemala pulls back one corner of a filthy mat hiding a tiny hole where the floor meets the wall and puts the money inside. "It's got to be worth our time, right?"

"*Our* time?" I say, feeling suddenly possessive about all that I've done. It's my journey, not Kemala's. Me who nearly died, not her. "I see you've got new clothes, too."

"Good spot. I look nice, huh?" She covers the hole, turns to me, and now her eyes are the knife. "You'd still be lying on your back if not for me, Tono. You'd still be a nothing. I helped you back from that coma. I told you stories in your sleep, cleaned you up. I *bothered* with you."

"You don't think I've done anything for myself? I should've died, but I came back to life."

"I've made deals for you so you can live better. *Be* better."

My mouth feels dry. "How much are you taking for yourself?" I ask.

"What are you, the police now?"

It's a good question. What am I, now, in this scummy little room? Tin Boy, the superhero, saving lives – so long as the price is right, so long as Kemala says it's all right. Is that who I've become?

The feelings are too big for this place. I feel smothered, suffocated. I picture my dad as the muddy sand buried him. He was the one man I'd have given anything to save, but I couldn't. I couldn't even look at him as he ...

Like him, suddenly I'm not there.

I'm outside, running. I grab the bike, swinging myself onto it as I push down on the pedals. I squeak and creak back the way I came. The guys with the skateboard step out to block the way.

"What's your rush, kid?" Gold Chain calls out to me. "What'd you do? Hey, I'm talking ..."

I keep going, straight for him, but swerve aside at the last second, the same moment that Gold Chain leaps away. But his friend is fast and kicks the skateboard into the bike. It hits the back wheel and gets caught in the bent spokes. I'm thrown forward, head first, hands stinging against the dusty pavement. And the red stone jumps from my pocket, skitters over the baked earth and then lies as still as I do.

The men have seen it.

"You're that one they're talking about," Bandana Man says. "That Tin Boy kid who thinks he's a superhero."

"And that must be the jewel he's been flashing around," Gold Chain says. "Got to be worth something."

I don't say anything.  I just spring up, grab
my stone and run.

There's a torrent of angry swear words
from behind me, pelting footsteps and the whiz
of little wheels over the tarmac.

They're coming after me.

I run headlong into the road, out in front of a bus, which blares its horn as I speed by. The noise is like wind at my back, pushing me on. The stone seems to pulse in my palm, and I feel strong. I reach the rubbish tip and run across mounds of stinking trash. My feet sink into the filth, but it doesn't matter, and it means the skateboard can't follow. And the two men can't sprint as fast as I can. I'm outrunning them, making for the tangle of yellowing palms and banana trees that border the tip. I can lose these idiots in the forest beyond.

Of course I can. I'm Tin Boy, aren't I?

But the scrawny trees are not the front of a forest. They stand in a line, only three deep in the grey sandy soil. I know that the mining companies have to plant new forest behind them, regenerating the land they've ruined once they move on. But the good soil has been washed away by the mining. Only the dead mud is left behind and nothing grows well. I look around at the grey dunes and turquoise pools, the craters and the used pits that stand deserted in this moon-like landscape. Are Gold Chain and Bandana Man following me? If they are, they'll be here soon.

The way ahead slopes upwards, a grey hillside I can't see past. A huge circular crater lies in my way – maybe forty metres across and filled with old, filthy water. I could take the long way around, past the open pits, but it's further and the men will surely see me. So, I go the quick way. I step off the side and drop down up to my neck in the stinking water, the surface black with flies. I have to swim to the far side.

It's then I realise that once I climb out I'll leave wet tracks in the sand. An advert for just where I'm hiding.

Then it hits me: it doesn't have to be an advert. I can make it a lure!

Bandana Man and Gold Chain think I'm running scared. I can leave a plain path of wet footprints over the hill for them to follow – and while they do that I'll circle round, double back behind them, grab the bike from where I left it and get away.

The plan's on. Scared, excited, I scramble over the rim. I crab-walk over the sand along the steep edge to get back round. By the time the two guys realise where my tracks are leading, it'll be too late to stop me ...

It should've been a good plan, but there's just one problem. While Gold Chain takes the crater pool like I did, Bandana Man doesn't want his Nikes wet, so runs around it. And the ground is higher there, so he sees my head bob over the ridge.

And suddenly he's shouting, charging my way.

Bandana Man's too fast for me. He grabs hold of my arm, pulling me over the ridge. We struggle and he punches me in the chest. I fall backwards, lash out with my leg, knock his feet from under him. Then I roll over and try to scramble back up. No good. Bandana Man kicks my ankle and I lose my footing and trip, rolling and sliding down a slope into one of the old pits. Sand clings to my wet skin and clothes, but maybe it slows me down so much that I land on two feet, unharmed. Panting, shaking, I look around me. The sides of the pit are maybe ten metres deep, except for the back wall, which stands a good three metres higher.

There are no braces to hold up the sides. My father died in a pit just like this one. Now it's me at the bottom of it.

# CHAPTER 13

# The Tin-Plated Truth

Bandana Man is peering over the sandy sides of the pit and is soon joined by Gold Chain, who is dripping wet and looking mad.

"Throw that red stone to us," Bandana Man calls. "We might not break your face."

I say nothing. I'm too scared. I can hear Dad's voice in my ears: "*Longsor!*" That last desperate shout for help before the mud crushed him.

"Don't make us come down there," Gold Chain warns me.

I stare up, dumb, as both men start scrambling into the pit.

Then I see it.

At the very top of the tall back wall of the pit, sand has started showering in.

"Back.  Get back!" I pant, pointing up. "*Longsor!*"

They see it.  The sandfall, gusting in like it's drawn to my call.  I'm still clutching the stone, and I look at it now, holding it up to the sun where it seems to glow.

"No way," Bandana Man says, suddenly rigid.  "He's making the pit fall in."

"On himself?" Gold Chain sneers.  "Why would he—?"

"Tin Boy survived the last landslide, didn't he?"

I'm doing it. Feelings flood into me. I'm actually doing this! I *do* have powers, no doubt now. I'll save these stupid thugs; I'll save myself. "Go!" I wheeze as the sand falls more hesitantly. "Go on, get out of here, before I bury you!"

I yell after them, but Bandana Man and Gold Chain are already scrambling away. Soon they're over the edge and I can't see them any more. The falling sand has stopped. Trembling, triumphant, I turn to the shallowest side, furthest from the tallest wall, and I climb out too.

It's then that I hear the laughter from behind the falling sand. High-pitched laughter with a hoarse edge.

"Ha!" Kemala says, standing up and crowing at the top of the hill. "Am I a genius? Yes!"

I'm staring at her, still pumped. I don't get it. "Did you see the sand?" I tell her. "I made it fall ..."

"You know this little trick's gonna spread your fame further than ever, Tin Boy." Kemala holds up Bandana Man's skateboard like a trophy and laughs again. "The best part of it is, I used that guy's stupid skateboard to shovel the sand down over you."

I feel suddenly cold. "You mean, *you* started that sandfall just now ...?"

"You're welcome," Kemala replies. "Those guys would've messed you up, Tono. Taken your stone. We can't have a superhero losing the stone that gives him his powers, right?" She shakes her head and climbs down to join me. "You're lucky I heard them chase after you. They're the ones who framed my aunt's friend – who got her arrested instead of them. They'd have hurt you bad."

"You could've buried me," I whisper. "Killed me."

"If I hadn't chanced it, they'd have killed you instead." Kemala shrugs. "They're bound to tell people. I've just upped your rep again. You'll get more bookings, more money." She pokes me in the chest. "I told you, you're welcome."

"'Again'?" I repeat, feeling sick, my heart skittering. "Just how did you up my rep last time?"

"The old woman's dream where she saw the pit fall in on her sons. I had to make it come true, didn't I? So she'd pay up. So word would get round."

My eyes are narrowing. I remember how wet and muddy Kemala looked that day. I whisper, "What the hell did you do?"

"I took some stuff from the other miners, buried a hosepipe in the sand and pumped water into the top of the pit. Made it easier to knock it in."

I close my eyes and wish I could shut my ears to Kemala. "And then you cleared your stuff away when we were trying to get Aldan out?"

"That's right.  And I fetched his mum," Kemala replies.

"But Aldan's leg – you could've killed him!"  A part of me is clinging to the hope that Kemala is joking around.  But, no, I remember her vanishing from the top of the pit, then reappearing with Aldan's mother so the woman could gratefully hand over whatever little money she had … "How much did she really pay?" I ask.  "I gave you twenty-five cents from my dollar, but I bet you took more, didn't you?"

"I needed it."  Kemala huffs, impatient.
"I had to pay people to go out and talk about the Tin Boy on every street corner.  Spread the word.  It worked too.  I told you, we have bookings …"

Kemala keeps talking, but I've turned and I'm walking away.  Not in the direction of Gold

Chain and Bandana Man; I can't face them again. I feel crushed. No power left in me. The truth hits me like a sledgehammer and as bare as the dead dunes all around. There never was any power. Tin Boy is just Tono. Scrawny little Tono, the idiot who actually believed he could be someone incredible.

"C'mon, where are you going?" Kemala shouts after me. "Those guys think you can control the sand! You're made, Tin Boy! People will pay. They'll pay!"

I walk on across the dustbowl, my feet squelching in my sandy plimsolls. Water has stuck the silt and mud to my skin and my clothes. You can't tell what colour these shorts are any more. It's like I'm part of this landscape. Inside and out.

# CHAPTER 14

# No Home

I find myself reaching the beach, and I sit down in the sand for hours, looking at the dredging ships out at sea. Their sides gleam in the afternoon sunlight, and the smoke and hum of their distant generators is like a giant cloud of flies over the ocean. I turn the red stone in my filthy fingers. I should wash myself off, but I don't want the sea to touch me. Not ever again.

The sun sinks and my feet take me home in the end. I don't want to face Rustam and Yan, but they're not going anywhere.

I know things are wrong the moment I step inside and see the empty beer bottles lying on the floor.

Rustam rises from his carpeted crate. I see my mattress on its side in Yan's room. My money was hidden beneath that, along with my comics. Oh god, this isn't good.

"You're back," Rustam announces. His dark eyes stick me to the wall. I know the signs: he's been drinking enough that he could hurt me and still sober enough to do it well.

"Where's Yan?" I ask Rustam.

"Out selling what we got today. It was a good day." Rustam raises his bottle to me and then takes a deep swig. "What did you do while we were working, Tono?"

"I sat on the beach."

"You went to see that one-armed freak."

I take a step towards my room. "I'm tired," I say. "I want to go to sleep."

"Want to count your money, maybe?" Rustam digs into his pocket and throws my coins down on the floor. They bounce and sparkle in the light of the bare bulb. I feel my heart sinking and hold my breath, waiting for Rustam's smirk to shrink or grow into whatever's coming next.

"How did you get it?" he asks.

"I earned it."

"Earned it how?" Rustam nods encouragingly. "Come on, Tono. Tell me how." He waits for me to speak, but not for long. "Only these two young punks have been telling a story all across town about a skinny boy called the Tin Jackass or something. A skinny boy who can start and stop landslides. A skinny boy who says his name is Rustam."

I lower my head. Find myself counting the coins on the floor. Soon, I know, I'll be counting the cost.

"That's how I heard, you see, Tono?" Rustam says. "Someone told me as we came ashore. This skinny boy used my name instead of his own. Imagine that."

"Uncle, please listen to me. Kemala had this idea that I—"

"Oh, so it was all the girl's fault, was it? Tono the big superhero, blaming a one-armed freak—"

"She's not a freak," I break in.

"Don't you dare speak over me!" Rustam throws his beer down and the bottle shatters, sending a little foaming tide across the floor. "You've been conning people with that freak, taking their money and keeping it from me. Me! The man who took you in when no one else would.  Who fed you, put a roof over you.  Who saved you."

I've never seen Rustam this mad.  "Uncle, please," I beg.  "I was waiting till I had more money and then—"

"You think I'm one of those mugs who believe you can turn back sand?  That I believe any crap that flops out of your mouth?" Rustam shakes his head and wipes his lips with the back of his hand.  "I paid for your god-damned doctors so you wouldn't die like your father, and for what?  So you can steal from your family?"

"I was saving it up for my mum," I shout at him.  "So she'll come back from Belitung with Rinal.  *They're* my family!"

"You clueless little runt."  Rustam laughs, but his eyes are still murderous.  "Your mother never went to Belitung.  She's barely an hour's drive from here, in Pangkal Pinang."

I stare at him. The words stick in my head; I can't process them. "Why?" I say at last. "Why would she—?"

"She left to marry a businessman who already had a son and didn't want another," Rustam tells me. He shakes his head. "Her family never liked your father, his head always in the clouds – till it ended up buried in the sand. They set it all up for her."

"You're lying." I'm shaking, and I think I might be sick. "Mum would never—"

"She did and she has and she's never coming back for you," Rustam says, his voice dropping lower. "We tried to spare you this, Tono, but it's better you know. Better you stop believing in impossible things, like saving people. Like superheroes." Rustam stalks across to my room, splashing in the spilled beer, and snatches up my comics from the floor. Then he rounds on me and snarls, "These stupid old rags. They filled your dad's head with stupid dreams that never came true, and they've done the same to you."

I want to say something, anything, but the words have dried like sand in my throat.

"Stupid!" Rustam shouts as he scrunches up the comics in his hands and starts to rip them apart. "Stupid, stupid!"

I scream and lunge for the comics, but he elbows me in the face and I reel back, slapping against the wall. My head's thick and throbbing, but I see Rustam stamping the coloured pages into the beer and broken glass on the floor, tearing up those priceless panels, balling them like they're trash. I fly at Rustam, knocking him over. He lands heavily on the floor and shouts out. When he sits up, I see that his arm's sliced open. He groans, presses a page against the bloody flap and Spidey disappears under a thick, dark stain.

"You ever come back here," Rustam whispers, clutching his arm, "I'll kill you. Hear me, Tono? I'll kill you."

Blood and sweat drip down into my eyes as I turn from him and face the black night outside on shaking legs.

And I go.

# CHAPTER 15

# Impossible Things

I walk and I walk in the dark.  The moon's tight with its light tonight, and so all the things I've tried not to think about for so long run about in the black.  And I think I see them in the red glow from my seabed stone: Dad's twisted body being pulled from the sand and mud; Rustam looming over Dad's casket; Mum leaving with Rinal, on the steps of the bus; the way Mum cried when she told me she'd see me soon.

By the time the sun appears, I'm outside Kemala's door. She's lying on the floor, using her new clothes as a pillow.

"You're back," she says, and pushes herself up on one elbow. "I knew you'd see sense."

"I only want my cut," I tell her. "Give me my share of the money you got trying to sell Tin Boy."

"I didn't try. I did sell you."

"No. Not me." I feel the red stone in my pocket, sticky with sand. "You sold Tin Boy."

Kemala goes to get the money from her hiding place. "I hope you don't feel bad about this, Tono. You shouldn't. So many people die scavenging for tin, so many get hurt. Kids and old folk and everyone in between – so many scared people every day. Tin Boy will give them comfort."

"He'll *sell* them comfort," I say. "Until the next accident."

"Maybe that accident won't happen. Not for ages, anyway. Not till we've made a fortune." Kemala leans down into the gap under the mat and her half-formed fingers push coins into her palm. "I mean, you *are* lucky, Tono. Look how you brought luck to me. You can bring it to everyone who has to work the mines."

"Wouldn't it be better if we could just shut the mines down? If we could stop destroying our home and destroying ourselves just so the big companies can make smarter smartphones that people like us will never even see?"

"But that will never happen," Kemala says. "Good luck might." She presses the money into my hand; it's enough. "There's no point in dreaming impossible things, Tono."

"You're the second person to tell me that."

"We're right."

"No," I say as I slip the coins in my pocket. "Dreaming impossible things is the first thing we have to do, if we want the dreams to be possible some day."

I pull my other hand out of my pocket. I place my red stone – my "tinkanite" – in her fingers. I suppose it has changed me, in a way. It's changed everything.

Kemala stares at my treasure and asks, "Why are you giving me this?"

"You'll be able to find yourself a new Tin Boy if that's what you want. I'm leaving here."

"Where will you go?"

"Pangkal Pinang," I say. "For a start."

I leave Kemala then. Outside in the
sour-smelling street, the sun beats down, the
tarmac shimmering as I head back into town.

I've got a bus to catch.  I'm going to find my mum.  Hear the truth from her lips, not my uncle's.

And once I've ticked that one impossible thing off my list, maybe I can start dreaming about some more.

# Notes from the author

## Where did the name "Tin Boy" come from?

The very first Tin Boy was actually me when I was 11 and studying the periodic table in Science. I noticed that the chemical symbol for tin was Sn, the first and last letters of "Stephen", and my best friend Martin's name fitted the symbol for manganese (Mn), so we started the secret Periodic Club and gave ourselves the code names Tin Boy and Ganese Man. The club was short-lived but my code name lodged somewhere in my subconscious ...

## Why did you want to tell this story?

A few years back I was writing a comedy adventure called *Invisible Inc.* and had to research which metals go into making a mobile phone. I learned that tin is one of the most important components of modern technology because it's used as solder for the circuit boards – and that much of it is produced at a terrible cost both to the environment and to the people who mine it. The big companies that use the tin aren't always careful about where it comes from, and when I learned about the thousands of illegal tin miners in Indonesia, and how whole families, even children, would risk their lives scavenging in exhausted pits left behind by the official companies, the basics of Tono's story came into my head almost at once: his finding the stone in the bottom of a pit and believing he might have powers. I remembered my old code name Tin Boy and how it sounded like a slightly sad and desperate superhero, and that gave me the title. Working out the broader story took much longer.

## How much of the story is true?

Bangka Belitung is a real province, and so is the predicament of the illegal miners – details of the awful conditions, the poverty and the death rate are all true. Most of the people who produce the tin will never own any of the gadgets it goes into making. The environmental damage to

Bangka, its waters and reefs will take centuries to undo.

## What can be done?

Organisations such as Friends of the Earth have run campaigns to raise awareness of the issues around tin mining and some progress has been made in regulating the industry and encouraging the big tech companies to source their tin responsibly. But many people upgrade their phones and tablets far more often than they need to, trying to keep up with the latest trends – and tin is not recycled from old phones. You could consider keeping your devices till they stop working; repair, don't replace. Think of the lives risked – and even lost – that helped to get that phone into your hand.

Our books are tested
for children and young people by
children and young people.

Thanks to everyone who consulted on
a manuscript for their time and effort in
helping us to make our books better
for our readers.